THE ATTACKS OF SEPTEMBER 11, 2001

I SURVIVED

THE SINKING OF THE *TITANIC*, 1912

THE SHARK ATTACKS OF 1916

HURRICANE KATRINA, 2005

THE BOMBING OF PEARL HARBOR, 1941

THE SAN FRANCISCO EARTHQUAKE, 1906

THE ATTACKS OF SEPTEMBER 11, 2001

I SURVIVED

THE ATTACKS OF SEPTEMBER 11, 2001

by Lauren Tarshis

illustrated by Scott Dawson

Scholastic Inc.

NEW YORK   TORONTO   LONDON   AUCKLAND
SYDNEY   MEXICO CITY   NEW DELHI   HONG KONG

The characters and details in this book are based on true stories, but are intended to be fictional composites of actual people and events.

No part of this publication may be reproduced, stored in a retrieval system, or transmitted in any form or by any means, electronic, mechanical, photocopying, recording, or otherwise, without written permission of the publisher. For information regarding permission, write to Scholastic Inc., Attention: Permissions Department, 557 Broadway, New York, NY 10012.

ISBN 978-0-545-20700-3

Text copyright © 2012 by Lauren Tarshis
Illustrations copyright © 2012 by Scholastic Inc.
All rights reserved. Published by Scholastic Inc.
SCHOLASTIC and associated logos are trademarks and/or
registered trademarks of Scholastic Inc.

25 24 23 22 21   14 15 16 17/0

Printed in the U.S.A.   40
First printing, July 2012
Designed by Tim Hall

FOR JENNIE ROSS

THE ATTACKS OF SEPTEMBER 11, 2001

CHAPTER 1

TUESDAY, SEPTEMBER 11, 2001

8:46 A.M.

NEW YORK CITY, NEW YORK

A bright blue sky stretched over New York City.

It was the morning rush. Men and women hurried to work. Taxis, cars, and buses zoomed through the streets.

And then there was the plane.

Many people in Lower Manhattan heard it before they saw it — the screaming roar of jet engines.

The massive aircraft streaked through the sky, barely skimming over rooftops.

Up and down the sidewalks, people froze.

Eleven-year-old Lucas Calley wasn't supposed to be in Manhattan that day. His parents had no idea that he'd caught a train into the city, that he was there, on a crowded sidewalk, looking up as it all began.

Lucas watched, almost hypnotized, as the plane careened through the sky.

He'd never seen a plane flying so low.

It was so close he could read the letters on the tail: *AA*.

American Airlines.

Panicked questions swirled through his mind.

Was there something wrong with the plane?

Was the pilot sick? Lost? Confused?

Pull up! Lucas wanted to shout. *Go higher!*

But the plane kept getting lower.

And faster.

And now Lucas's heart stopped as he saw what was in the plane's path: the Twin Towers of the World Trade Center. The silver-and-glass buildings, each a quarter of a mile tall, rose high above the New York City skyline.

The plane sped up.

No!

With one last ferocious roar, the jet plunged into the side of one of the towers.

There was a thundering explosion.

People all around Lucas screamed.

And then the bright blue sky filled with black smoke and fire.

CHAPTER 2

WEDNESDAY, AUGUST 29, 2001
PORT JACKSON, NEW YORK
10:00 A.M.

As usual, football practice was brutal.

It was ninety-five degrees. Lucas was soaked in sweat. Three guys had already puked up their Gatorades. Lucas's body felt like one big bruise.

A football came sailing through the air. It looked like an impossible catch — Lucas's favorite kind. He took off, legs pumping, eyes on the ball. At exactly the right split second, he leaped up as high as he could, plucked the ball from the air, and grabbed it to his chest as he crashed to the ground.

All around him, guys hooted and cheered and high-fived.

A familiar happy feeling rushed over Lucas. Sure, his entire body ached. Yeah, Coach B. was always screaming at them. But this is where Lucas was happiest, where he belonged: on this broiling hot turf field with his football team, the Port Jackson Jaguars.

It had been Uncle Benny's idea that Lucas could be a football player. Benny was Dad's best friend from Ladder 177, the New York City firehouse where they both worked. Lucas had

always liked Uncle Benny — everyone did. Dad once said that Benny was like the firehouse cheerleader.

A six-foot-two-inch cheerleader with a shamrock tattoo.

But it wasn't until Lucas was in third grade that he really got close to Uncle Benny. That year,

Lucas's dad was badly hurt in a warehouse fire in Brooklyn. He was in the hospital burn center for almost two months. Uncle Benny practically moved in with Mom and Lucas until Dad was better. Lucas would wake up some mornings and find Uncle Benny reading the sports pages at the kitchen table. Before Lucas could say, "Where's Mom?" Uncle Benny would grab him by the arm and sit him down. "You gotta see this," he'd say, holding up a picture of some football player Lucas had never heard of.

Lucas would sit there, pretending to be interested. He'd never been a sports kid. He and Dad were always so busy working on their projects. Before Dad got hurt, they'd been spending every weekend in their basement workshop, building a model of the Ladder 177 truck, the Seagrave 75.

But Uncle Benny wasn't interested in truck models. What Uncle Benny loved was football.

And soon enough he had Lucas glued to *Monday Night Football*, cheering for Uncle Benny's teams, watching ESPN, and booing the players Uncle Benny hated. Uncle Benny bought Lucas a football, and then spent hours with him in the backyard, teaching him to throw and catch.

And then came the day when Uncle Benny appeared with the form to sign up for the Jaguars.

"I can't really play football," Lucas said.

Back then Lucas had been pudgy, shorter even than some of the girls in his grade.

But Uncle Benny got his mom and dad to sign the form. And the next thing Lucas knew, Uncle Benny was driving him to his first practice.

Lucas had to smile as he thought back to that day — he was a little butterball stuffed into his pads and brand-new cleats.

"I think we should go home," he said to Uncle Benny, choking back tears.

"No, you don't," Uncle Benny said. "You want to get out there and show what you can do!"

And Uncle Benny's eyes were so big and sparkling, like bright lights spelling out the words *You can do it!*

So Lucas did it.

And from that first day, Lucas felt like he'd found his place.

It wasn't really the game he loved. It was being on the team, being surrounded by the guys. They watched each other's backs. Winners or losers, they stuck together.

Uncle Benny had also taught him the secret of catching a football: that you had to *believe* you were going to catch it.

"You have to feel it in your heart," Uncle Benny said.

It worked every time.

Almost.

Toward the end of practice, someone threw another impossible pass.

"Go get it, Lucas!" the guys screamed.

And off Lucas went, his eyes glued to the ball, his arms stretched out so long he felt like he could grab the sun. But something went wrong. His heart knew he would catch it. But his ankle didn't.

It wobbled and Lucas lost his balance. Suddenly he was flying through the air, a missile out of control. He crashed headfirst into the hard turf.

Crack!

He could practically feel his brain smacking against the inside of his skull.

A white light of pain exploded inside Lucas's head.

He saw stars — a whole galaxy behind his eyes.

And then he blacked out.

CHAPTER 3

The next few hours were a blur. The guys swarming around him, Coach B. helping him off the field, the long wait at the emergency room, Mom's and Dad's worried faces.

But in the end, Lucas was fine.

He just had a concussion.

Sure, it was worse than the concussion he'd gotten during play-offs last season, and the one before that, during the summer after fourth grade. But he knew he would get better if he took it easy, just like the other times.

That night, Dad came into Lucas's room to check on him.

"Feeling okay?" he asked.

"I'm good, Dad," Lucas said.

He really was feeling much better.

What killed him was knowing he'd be off the field for twelve days.

He already missed the guys.

Looking up at Dad, Lucas saw a face almost exactly like his own — they even had the same specks of green in their brown eyes.

"You need anything?" Dad asked.

"I'm good," Lucas said again.

Lucas stayed very still, hoping Dad would stick around and talk.

But Dad stood up. He leaned over and kissed Lucas on the forehead.

And he was gone.

Lucas's heart sank a little.

There had been a time when Dad would have plopped himself down on Lucas's bed and announced his plan for their next adventure. Some nights back then, they'd wait for Mom to fall asleep so they could sneak down to the basement to work on the Seagrave.

Dad and Lucas had been a team — a team of two.

But then came the warehouse fire.

Two years had passed since it happened, but the memories were still sharp — the doorbell ringing in the middle of the night, the Chief and Uncle Benny standing in the doorway, still stinking of smoke. Mom's tears. And later, the sight of Dad wrapped in bandages, his face white with pain.

Lucas had always known that his dad's job was dangerous. Sometimes Dad would bring Lucas to the firehouse on his days off. Lucas would help with the chores — washing the truck, cooking lunch, checking the hoses. But what he loved most was sitting around the big, round kitchen table, listening to the guys talk about the fires they'd fought.

To Lucas, they were superheroes.

They ran into buildings filled with blazing orange flames and choking black smoke. They used metal spears to smash windows, rip out walls, and bash through doors. They carried people down oven-hot stairwells and dangled from ropes hundreds of feet in the air. The fires they tamed were more evil and ferocious than any video-game villain or movie monster.

But it wasn't until the warehouse fire that Lucas understood what a fire could do to a real man, a man like his dad.

Dad had never talked about what happened to him inside that warehouse. All Lucas knew was that four firemen died, and Dad was badly burned in an explosion. Even after all this time, the scars on Dad's arms were bright red and lumpy, like raw hamburger.

But the burns weren't the worst of what that fire did to Dad.

It took away his easy smile and booming laugh. It turned him quiet. Some days Dad barely talked at all. He'd get this look in his eyes, like his mind was somewhere else — probably sifting through the ashes in that warehouse.

Lucas stopped asking when they'd get back to that model of the Seagrave, which was half-finished and covered with dust in the basement. And when the memories of that night came back, or he started worrying that Dad would never be himself again, he'd close his eyes and imagine himself on the football field, surrounded by the guys, their voices calling out his name as he made one of his famous catches.

CHAPTER 4

Monday came, the last day before Lucas would be allowed back on the field. He'd been crossing out the days on his calendar, counting down. Mom picked him up early from school for a doctor's appointment — she wanted him checked out before he was cleared to play.

18

"I'm fine," Lucas said. "Can't you tell?"

Lucas lifted his arm and flexed his bicep.

Mom laughed. "You look incredible."

Mom had decided to take him to a new doctor. "I hear he's the best," she said. "We were lucky he could fit you in."

His name was Dr. Barrett. With his blond crew cut and huge shoulders, he looked more like a linebacker than a doctor.

Dr. Barrett brought Lucas into an exam room and checked him over — looking in his eyes, listening to his heart and lungs. He asked him to walk across the room with one foot in front of the other. Lucas was sure he passed all the tests.

After the exam, Dr. Barrett waved Mom and Lucas back into his office. The wall was covered with framed diplomas and pictures of football players. Lucas looked at a photo of a rough-looking man in a Denver Broncos uniform.

"That's Dan Brock," Dr. Barrett said. "Have you heard of him?"

The name was familiar, but Lucas didn't know why.

"He was All-American at the University of Wisconsin, then a third-round pick for the NFL."

Dr. Barrett pointed to the next photo in the row, a big smiling man with a busted-up nose and chubby baby cheeks.

"That's Tyrus Vallone," he said. "He was a star tackle at Florida State, and then he played ten years for Green Bay."

There were three other pictures on the wall. It was only the last one that Lucas recognized.

"Is that Stan Walsh? Didn't he . . . isn't he . . ."

He was dead.

He had died just a few months ago. Uncle Benny had been upset about it — he'd played against Stan Walsh when he was a college player.

Dr. Barrett nodded, seeing that Lucas knew about Stan Walsh. "He had just turned forty," the doctor said. "He had the same kind of brain disease you see in men in their eighties."

Dr. Barrett pointed up at the wall, at all of the players.

"All of those men are dead," he said. "They donated their brains to our lab, so we can study them. They all died because of concussions."

A chill ran up and down Lucas's spine.

He looked at Mom. Her eyes were wide with shock.

"We used to think concussions were like sprained ankles," Dr. Barrett said. "You get dinged, you let it heal, and you're good to go. But now we know that too many concussions can actually change the brain."

"How many concussions is too many?" Mom asked.

Lucas held his breath.

"I would say that in an eleven-year-old boy, three concussions in two years is too many."

The room was suddenly quiet. Lucas could feel the eyes of those football players looking down on him.

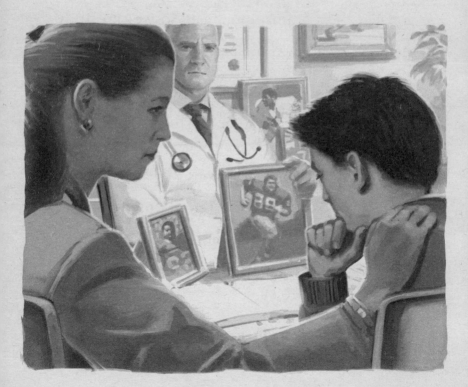

"I can stay out another week," Lucas said. It would be torture. But he'd be back in time for the first game.

"I'm sorry, Lucas," Dr. Barrett said. "But what I'm suggesting is that you never play football again."

All night Lucas argued and begged. He had a million reasons why that doctor was wrong, and he told Mom and Dad practically every single one.

When that didn't work, he offered to sit out for two more weeks — then three.

"Just please don't make me quit!"

Finally Dad put his hands on Lucas's shoulders.

"Lucas," Dad said in a soft voice. "Football is a game. I know you love it. But it is just a game."

A game.

Of course Lucas knew that.

But that game was the most important thing in his life.

What would he do without his team?

That night he lay awake in bed for hours, thinking.

It was past midnight when he realized what he needed to do.

He had to see Uncle Benny.

Before Mom and Dad talked to Coach. Before it was too late.

Dad left early the next morning. He was teaching a class at The Rock, the firefighter training school, across a bridge from Manhattan, on Randall's Island. Mom dropped Lucas off at the bus stop on her way to work.

The minute her car disappeared, Lucas sprinted back home. He grabbed his bike and pedaled as fast as he could to the train station.

He caught the 7:17 with one minute to spare.

Lucas knew how wrong this was — to skip school, to sneak into the city without Mom and Dad knowing.

But right then, none of that mattered.

He had to see Uncle Benny.

Somehow, Uncle Benny would make this right.

CHAPTER 5

TUESDAY, SEPTEMBER 11, 2001

8:15 A.M.

NEW YORK CITY, NEW YORK

Lucas had made this trip so many times with Dad he knew it by heart — the train to Penn Station, the subway to Canal Street.

When he got out of the subway, he looked up

and found his landmark: the two silver buildings jutting into the sky.

The Twin Towers of the World Trade Center.

The World Trade Center was nine blocks south of the fire station. So he just followed his view of the towers until he hit the right street.

As Lucas walked, he thought of the last time he and Dad visited the Trade Center. They'd gotten there early, before the observation deck was open. But the guard noticed Dad's FDNY hat and let them go up.

They had the place to themselves.

The view from the 110th floor was like looking down on Manhattan from a cloud. The whole island stretched out in front of them. The buildings below looked like toys, the rivers like trickling streams, the cars and trucks looked smaller than the models Lucas and Dad built in the basement.

They stood there, just Dad and Lucas, alone on top of the world.

That was right before the warehouse fire — only two years before now.

It seemed like a very long time ago.

When Lucas got to the firehouse, the garage door was open.

And there, right next to the Seagrave, was Uncle Benny.

He glanced up and gave an offhand smile, obviously thinking that Lucas was just a neighborhood kid hoping to get a peek at the truck.

But then Uncle Benny looked at Lucas again.

"Hey, you!" he said with a surprised grin, striding over.

He pulled Lucas into the garage.

Lucas breathed in the familiar smell of diesel fuel and sweat. He'd always loved the sight of all the guys' black bunker coats hanging on the walls, the pants already tucked into the big black boots.

The firehouse was crowded. The guys from the last shift were saying their good-byes and the morning men were just getting settled.

Guys came from all over the firehouse to say hi to Lucas, wrapping him in bear hugs, rubbing his head, and telling him he was growing like a weed.

"I've missed my assistant," said Georgie, who drove the truck and also did most of the cooking. On Lucas's visits with Dad, his favorite job was helping Georgie cook his famous tomato sauce.

Chief Douglas came over, his smile flashing from under his bushy gray mustache, followed by Mark, one of the youngest guys. He and his family lived not far from Lucas. His eight-year-old twin boys were football fanatics, and Mark coached their team. Last season they came to one of Lucas's games. Afterward, the twins had asked Lucas for his autograph.

Suddenly Uncle Benny looked around.

"Where's your pops?" he said. "He's already done at The Rock?"

Lucas shook his head.

"Your mom brought you?" Uncle Benny said.

Lucas shook his head again.

Uncle Benny eyed Lucas, and his smile faded.

"You okay?" he said softly.

Lucas didn't answer.

Uncle Benny looked at Georgie, who gave him a nod.

"Cover me, will you guys?" Uncle Benny asked. "I'll be back in a few."

Uncle Benny led Lucas outside and they started walking.

"This is some kind of day, isn't it?" he said, squinting up at the bright blue sky.

Neither of them said anything more, until finally Lucas came out with it.

"Mom and Dad are making me quit football," he said. "Because of my concussions."

Lucas watched Uncle Benny's face, waiting for his eyebrows to mash together in anger, for his cheeks to burn furious red.

But Uncle Benny just nodded.

Then he looked at Lucas. "I've been worried about you, kiddo," he said. "You've got yourself a darned good brain. I don't want you ending up like poor Stan Walsh."

And then it suddenly hit Lucas — it was Uncle Benny who got Mom to bring him to see Dr. Barrett! He must have known he'd been Stan Walsh's doctor.

Lucas had come all this way because he thought Uncle Benny would help him. And Uncle Benny was the reason he had to quit!

32

Uncle Benny stopped and put his hands on Lucas's shoulders. It seemed like he was trying to keep Lucas pinned to the ground, like otherwise he'd fly away. He stared at Lucas with those bright-light eyes of his.

"You'll find something else," he said.

What else do I have? Lucas wanted to ask.

But before he could, something over Lucas's shoulder caught Uncle Benny's attention. Lucas turned, and then he saw it too: a glint of silver against the bright blue.

Out of nowhere, a huge jet airplane zoomed into view.

It was flying very low.

CHAPTER 6

8:46 A.M.

"What the —" Uncle Benny said.

He and Lucas stood and watched as the plane tore through the sky, its engine screaming.

Everyone else on the sidewalk stopped and looked up.

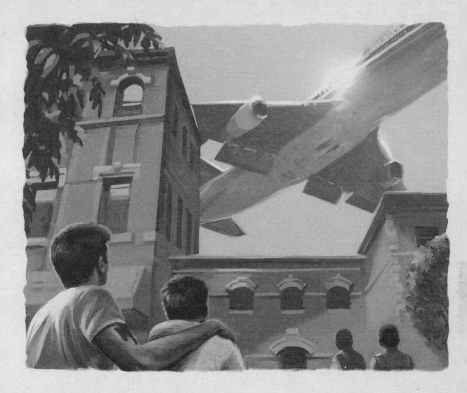

Lucas had never seen an airplane flying so low, except taking off or landing.

He could see the plane so clearly — the engines tucked under the wings, the sun glinting off the windows. He could even read the letters on the tail: *AA*.

American Airlines.

The engines roared.

That plane had to be in trouble. It was going to crash!

Questions raced through Lucas's mind.

Had the plane's instruments broken? Was the pilot confused? Was he sick? Once Lucas heard about a pilot who had a heart attack in the middle of a flight.

But that didn't make sense. There would be a copilot there to take over.

Or maybe airplanes flew like this all the time in New York City, and Lucas just hadn't noticed before? Or no, it had to be a movie. That was it! Some action movie was being filmed over New York City.

But where were the cameras? How were they filming the plane?

Something was wrong. And everyone knew it. People up and down the sidewalk were stopped in their tracks, hypnotized by the sight of a jet ripping across the sky.

The plane turned slightly, one wing dipping down. The engine's roar turned to a screech. It was moving faster now, and going lower and lower. It barely missed the tops of some buildings as it careened through the air.

But just ahead, two buildings stood taller than the rest: the Twin Towers.

The plane was heading right for one of the towers.

Turn! Lucas wanted to scream. *Pull up!*

But it didn't turn. And suddenly, the plane plunged like a knife into the side of one of the buildings.

For a split second, Lucas waited for the plane

to reappear on the other side, to keep flying as though nothing had happened.

But then,

Kaboom!

A gigantic fireball — orange and black — exploded out of the side of the building.

Lucas jumped back in horror.

All around him, people screamed.

Black, fiery smoke gushed out of a huge gash in the building's side, billowing into the sky.

Lucas turned away. He couldn't look anymore.

He looked at Uncle Benny instead.

Uncle Benny was already shouting into his phone.

"Call dispatch . . . a plane just crashed into the World Trade Center! This is a 10-60 . . . yes, a 10-60!"

10-60 was the worst kind of alarm.

And that's when it hit Lucas: There had to be hundreds of people trapped in that tower. And no matter how dangerous it was, firefighters like Dad and Uncle Benny were going to try to save them.

CHAPTER 7

"It looks like Tower One," Uncle Benny was saying, his phone pressed to his ear as he and Lucas ran back to the firehouse. "The North tower . . . no, not a small plane. It was a jet. A big jet. Yes, I'm sure." Uncle Benny was shouting now. "I saw it with my own eyes!"

Lucas kept glancing back, each time hoping that the tower would be magically healed.

But each time he looked, there was more and more black smoke.

The sound of sirens filled the air.

"Get ready," Uncle Benny was saying. "We're going to need everything we have. There has to be at least ten floors of fire."

Ten floors of fire.

Dad had told Lucas that every floor of the Twin Towers was about the size of a football field. Lucas tried to imagine what ten football fields would look like — each one on fire.

How many firefighters would it take to put those fires out?

And what if each of those fires was almost a quarter mile in the air?

That's how high the towers were.

Lucas knew how much firefighters hated high-rises. Elevators were usually too dangerous to use in a fire. They could stop working suddenly and fill up with smoke. But the only other choice was to lug heavy hoses and fifty pounds of gear up endless flights of stairs.

Georgie once told Lucas that it could take two minutes for a firefighter to walk up just one flight of stairs. Lucas looked back at the tower. That fire was near the top — maybe the eightieth or nintieth floor. That meant it could be two hours before firefighters could get there.

Could the people on those floors wait that long for help?

The Seagrave was already out of the garage when Lucas and Uncle Benny got back to the firehouse. Georgie was at the wheel. Men from both shifts were piled on.

Benny ran over to grab his turnout clothes and helmet. Lucas followed after him.

"Uncle Benny?" he said. "What will you do?"

Uncle Benny stepped into his bunker pants and boots.

"We'll do what we always do," he said.

He put his hand on Lucas's head for a moment, then ran to the truck.

Chief Douglas called out to Lucas from the truck.

"Your dad is heading to the scene," he said. "You sit tight!"

"Take care of things for us, buddy," Uncle Benny said.

The truck pulled away, its siren wailing. The garage door shut.

And Lucas stood there, in shock. Alone.

He ran to the phone and called Mom.

She didn't answer.

He left a message, struggling to keep his voice

from cracking — that he was at the firehouse, that he was fine. That she should call him.

He hung up and stood there, his mind spinning.

Uncle Benny's words whispered in his head.

We'll do what we always do.

What they always did.

Fight fires. Save people's lives.

Yes, that's what they'd do now.

The FDNY was the biggest fire department in the world.

They were the best.

And they would do what they always did.

CHAPTER 8

9:00 A.M.

Dad once told Lucas that what he liked most about fighting fires was that everyone had a job to do.

"If you don't work together, you don't put out the fire."

Now, Lucas looked around the firehouse. He

needed a job, he realized. Something he could do to help.

He went into the kitchen.

The table was covered with plates of half-eaten bacon and eggs. The sink was overflowing with dirty pots.

He got to work, clearing the dishes and glasses from the table.

Every few minutes the alarm box squawked, and the dispatcher came on with a new alarm.

"All units meet at Vesey and West streets. . . ."

The TV was on the counter, the sound turned down. The picture on the screen showed the burning tower. Lucas reached out and turned the volume up so he could hear it over the voice of the dispatcher.

"If you're just joining us, ladies and gentlemen," the TV man's voice said, "you're looking at an extraordinary sight. Just a few minutes ago, a plane crashed into Tower One at New York's famed World Trade Center. We have no official information about what kind of plane it was, but witnesses report it was a commercial jet."

Lucas picked up Georgie's huge cast-iron skillet and started scrubbing.

"The towers were built in 1970," the man continued. "At 110 floors each, they were once the tallest buildings in the world. There are hundreds of firefighters on the scene. We have reports that firefighters have been entering the building and heading up the stairs to reach people who might need assistance. It's an amazing sight."

The smoke was thicker now, painting the blue sky a dirty brown. There were white dots floating in the smoke — almost like confetti.

Paper, Lucas realized. Millions of pieces of paper, swept out through the hole in the building.

The man kept talking about the towers — that

they took four years to build, that they could withstand winds of 140 miles per hour, that 50,000 people worked there.

His voice was calm, almost like a teacher giving a history lesson.

Lucas was reaching up to hang the heavy skillet on the hook over the sink.

Suddenly the man on the TV gasped.

"Oh, my God! What was that? Another explosion! Ladies and gentlemen — it looks like a second plane . . . yes, another jet. It has just crashed into the second tower."

The heavy skillet slipped out of Lucas's hand and into the sink, shattering plates and glasses. Lucas barely noticed. His eyes did not move from the TV screen.

"Ladies and gentlemen," the man said again, his voice shaking. "We're going to replay the video of what we just saw. . . ."

The screen flipped. It showed the North Tower burning. And then suddenly, on the left side of the screen, another plane appeared. Just like the first, it was a big jet. And quick as a blink, it slammed into the other tower, exploding into a fireball.

Fire erupted out of all sides of the building, a ring of flaming blackness. Now there were two clouds of churning black smoke.

Lucas's heart pounded. It was hard to breathe.

There were more people talking on the TV now, not just the man.

"Oh my . . . oh my . . . that looked . . ." one woman said.

"What did we just see?" said another.

"Ladies and gentlemen," the man said. "We have just witnessed the horrific sight of a second plane hitting the other tower — the South Tower. . . . There was a massive explosion."

"There must be a computer problem, a complete failure of the air traffic control system," said the first woman.

What the man said next made Lucas's entire body start to shake.

"That did not look like an accident," he said. "It looks like that plane flew into that tower on purpose. I think this is some kind of attack."

CHAPTER 9

Lucas tried calling Mom again. Now when he called he got a fast busy signal and a recording.

"All circuits are busy."

He tried Dad's phone. Same thing. He dialed over and over — Mom, Dad, Mom, Dad. He just kept getting the busy signal.

The department radio crackled.

"Recall, recall," the dispatcher said. *"All*

personnel, on duty and off, are to report. I repeat. This is a recall of all emergency personnel."

There were 11,000 firefighters in the department.

They needed every single one.

Before Lucas knew what he was doing, he had run out into the street.

He couldn't be alone, watching the world fall apart on TV.

He needed to find Dad, and Uncle Benny, and the rest of the men.

He wanted to be with them.

He knew he wasn't thinking clearly.

He didn't know if he'd even be able to get close to where they were, if it was even safe to try.

But he went anyway.

Some kind of attack.

Some kind of attack.

Was that man on TV right?

What did that even mean?

Who was attacking?

Did he mean that those planes had hit the towers *on purpose*?

The thought hadn't even come into Lucas's mind when he saw the first plane hit. But thinking about it now, of course that was the only thing that made sense.

The day was so perfectly clear. There was no way that two airplanes could have hit the towers unless they had been aiming right for them.

But who could be insane enough, evil enough, to fly planes into buildings?

Lucas wiped away the tears running down his face.

He wove through the crowds of people on the sidewalk. Some were running north. But most seemed like they were in shock, standing there dazed, staring at the fires above them.

The only noise was sirens — hundreds of them — honking and screaming, wailing and shrieking and blaring. The sounds all crashed together into one terrible song.

A crowd of people huddled around something in the middle of the street. Lucas slowed down and looked — it was a big tire attached to a tangle of metal.

It didn't look like the tire of a car or a truck.

"What is that?" a woman said.

"It's part of a plane," said a man. "It's landing gear."

Lucas looked away.

He pushed through the crowd, heading south.

Vesey and West streets.

That's where the staging area was, where the firefighters were gathering.

If Dad had made it here from Randall's Island, that's where Lucas would find him. He would look for the Seagrave. He would wait there for Dad.

Lucas inched through the crowd. Most people were standing still, watching. But now there were more people coming from the direction of the towers. Some of them were soaked in sweat, their clothes tattered. But it was the looks on their faces — stunned and horrified — that told Lucas where they had come from: inside the towers.

There were dozens and dozens of them, some walking alone, others holding hands. Some of the women were barefoot. He imagined their high-heeled shoes kicked into the corners of the stairwells. Nobody was carrying a purse or a briefcase. And Lucas understood why; he'd heard many stories about people who had survived fires and explosions and collapses. So many times they'd escaped with not a second to spare. If they had stopped for anything — to grab a purse or tie a shoe — they wouldn't have made it.

A policeman up ahead was trying to stop people from moving south.

"Everyone please leave this area!" he shouted. "It's not safe. Please leave this area and head north!"

But Lucas kept walking, and nobody tried to stop him. He felt invisible.

Ladder 177 had to be one of the first units to get to the towers. That meant they'd be the closest. Lucas was still three blocks away when he felt a hand on his shoulder.

"Hey," a young policeman said. "Where are you going? Are you lost?"

"I need to find . . ."

And before he could get the words out, he heard someone calling his name.

"Lucas!"

His name rose up over all of the sirens.

"Dad!"

And there was his dad, pushing through the crowd.

He grabbed Lucas and held him tight.

For a few seconds, Lucas couldn't hear the sirens.

All he could hear was the beating of Dad's heart.

CHAPTER 10

9:50 A.M.

Dad told Lucas that he'd driven to Manhattan from Randall's Island as soon as the first plane hit.

"I was going to head right to the scene," Dad said. "But I got the message that you were at the

59

firehouse. So I went there first. Chief said you'd be waiting for me."

"I'm sorry," Lucas said. "I just couldn't stay . . . I . . ."

Dad held up his hand.

There was no time to talk. And Lucas got the idea that nothing that had happened before this morning mattered anymore — not now, maybe not ever again.

"We need to find the guys," Dad said. "I need to get my gear from the truck. And then I'm going to find someone to take you back to the firehouse."

Lucas didn't want to go back there. But he didn't argue.

"They're not going to be able to put the fires out," Dad said. "This is a rescue operation now. We just want to get all of the people out of there."

Dad's walkie-talkie crackled. Muffled voices mixed with static came through.

Dad kept switching channels, trying to hear. He swore under his breath.

"Nobody can talk to anyone," he said. "These radios have never worked. And now people are totally shut off. Nobody can get through to the men in the towers."

They passed a pickup truck. The back was completely smashed, and a jet engine, still smoking, sat on the ground just behind it. The driver's door was open — someone had been in the car when it was hit and had gotten away.

"Lucky," Dad said as he pulled Lucas along, past the truck. One mile per hour slower and the entire cab would have been crushed.

There were people sitting on the sidewalks being treated by paramedics. Some were in bad shape. Lucas tried to keep his eyes straight ahead.

A woman staggered up to Dad. Her gray hair was soaked with sweat. Her face was bright red with streaks of black under her eyes. She was breathing very hard, her hand on her chest.

"Can you help me?" she gasped. "My heart. I came down the stairs. . . . My friends . . . I don't know where they are. . . . There was so much smoke. . . ."

Lucas knew Dad didn't want to stop — he wanted to find his crew.

"Okay," Dad said in a low and gentle voice. "Don't worry. We're going to get you what you need."

He turned to Lucas, pointing to an ambulance a few yards away. "Tell one of the paramedics we need help here."

Lucas ran over and told one of the paramedics, then hurried back to sit with Dad and the woman. Dad kept talking to her while they waited. He introduced himself and asked for her name, and about her family. The woman was gripping Dad's arm so tightly that her fingernails were digging into his skin. Dad didn't budge. He kept talking to her, trying to calm this person he'd never met and would probably never see again.

Finally the paramedics came. A minute later they had the woman on a stretcher and into the ambulance.

Dad and Lucas continued their search for Ladder 177.

But suddenly there was a deep roaring noise. The ground trembled.

Dad stopped short. He looked around.

His eyes flew up.

He grabbed Lucas by the arm and shouted.

"Run!"

Lucas had no idea what was happening. But

suddenly there was the loudest noise he'd ever heard. Louder than a hundred freight trains. Louder than all those sirens.

"What is it?" Lucas cried, his voice cracking with terror.

Dad pulled Lucas along, shouting, *"Run! Run!"* to the people all around.

Dad kept looking over his shoulder, pulling Lucas harder, urging him to move faster.

They came to a convenience store and Dad pushed the door open.

He threw Lucas inside and then called to people just behind them.

"In here!" he called. "Hurry! Hurry!"

Just a few people followed. Then Dad slammed the door shut.

"Everyone get down! Cover your heads!"

Lucas dove to the ground and then —

Whoosh!

There was the sound of shattering glass and a powerful blast of hot wind.

Minutes passed. Lucas squeezed his eyes shut and covered his ears. His mouth and nose filled with gritty dust. It was hard to breathe.

If he hadn't known better, he would have been sure that he was in the middle of a tornado — a boiling hot tornado.

And suddenly the noise and wind stopped.

There was silence.

Lucas opened his eyes, but he couldn't see anything.

All around was pure darkness.

For a long moment he was pretty sure the world had ended.

And that he was the only person left on Earth.

CHAPTER 11

It was Dad's voice that broke the silence.

"Lucas!" Dad shouted.

"Dad," Lucas rasped, spitting dust from his mouth.

"Is anyone hurt?" Dad called.

People coughed and hacked and sniffed. But nobody seemed to be badly hurt.

Dust was everywhere. It coated Lucas, every

inch of him. It was in his nose, between his teeth, stuck to his tongue and to the back of his throat. It wasn't like regular dust. Some of the grains were jagged — bits of ground glass. When Lucas tried to brush himself off, the dust cut into his skin.

"I have a light," Dad said in a calm and quiet voice. "I'm going to turn it on. Follow the light and come to me. We're going to stay together. We're all going to be all right."

There was a click, and then the glow of a small yellow circle. It looked like the moon on a foggy night. The air was filled with white floating dust — to Lucas it seemed like they were trapped inside a snow globe.

There were four other people in the store with him and Dad, two women and two men. The younger of the men came from behind the counter of the store. He worked there.

Dad asked everyone their names.

"I want everyone to put a piece of clothing in front of your mouth," he told them. "It's not good to breathe this dust."

Lee, the store worker, got big bottles of water for everyone, and rolls of paper towels. Everyone rinsed their mouths. Dad soaked a paper towel and carefully washed Lucas's eyes and face, then he helped the others. Catherine, the younger of the two women, was crying. The other people comforted her.

"What *was* that?" Catherine sobbed. "Was there another plane? Someone said there was another plane."

"No," Dad said. "That was not a plane. I think the top part of the building must have come down."

The door was stuck. Dad kicked out the jagged glass that clung to the door frame.

He stepped out first, then turned to help everyone through, out of the store.

Dad had told them he wanted to move quickly.

The four strangers started walking, holding hands.

But Dad stopped just outside the store, his hand clamped to Lucas's shoulder, staring at the scene of destruction all around them. It seemed to be much worse south of them, where even through the fog of dust, Lucas could see that twisted steel beams and big chunks of concrete filled the streets.

Cars were on fire. Fire trucks and ambulances were smashed. A few weak sirens squawked. It sounded like the trucks were crying for help.

All around them, people climbed out of windows and doorways. Everyone was coated with the white dust.

Lucas thought of a book he'd read on World

War II last year. There were pictures of cities that had been bombed and burned to the ground.

That's what this scene reminded him of — war.

Dad was looking intently south, like he was searching for something.

"It's gone," he said in a soft voice that only Lucas could hear.

"What's gone?" Lucas said.

"One of the towers," Dad said. "The entire building collapsed."

Nothing around them looked like the wreckage of a collapsed 110-story building. Where were the big hunks of glass and steel, the smashed office furniture and computers, the miles of wires and pipes?

"Where is it?" Lucas said.

There was nothing but dust.

"It's all around us," Dad said.

The dust, Lucas realized. That *was* the tower. It was practically all that was left.

Lucas tried not to think about how many people might still be in the buildings — the men and women working there, the hundreds of fire-fighters and police and paramedics who were on the scene.

Georgie and Mark.

Uncle Benny.

Lucas tried not to think about the people who might have been in that building when it came down.

Dad would have been — if he hadn't come looking for Lucas in the firehouse.

Dad took Lucas's hand and held it tight.

"We need to move fast," he said.

The other tower, Lucas realized. If the first one could fall, the second one could, too.

And so they began their march north, Dad and Lucas together.

The dust cleared as they reached Chambers Street.

All of a sudden the world was bright again.

But it didn't matter, Lucas realized.

It didn't matter how far they walked, or how much time went by.

Nothing would ever be the same again.

CHAPTER 12

SUNDAY, NOVEMBER 4, 2001

2:15 P.M.

The air was crisp and chilly. Lucas stood at the edge of the field.

The sounds of football filled the air — the cheers of the crowd, the trill of the ref's whistle, the laughs of little kids playing tag in front of the snack bar.

Mom and Dad were up in the bleachers. They waved at him.

He waved back.

A player ran off the field for a drink of water.

"Hey, Lucas!" he said.

It was James, one of Mark's twins — Lucas had finally learned to tell them apart.

"Hey, buddy," Lucas said. "Great game."

The little boy smiled up through his face mask.

Lucas held out his hand to high-five and the kid gave it a good whack.

James ran back out on the field.

Lucas turned, hoping James didn't see the tears in his eyes.

He just needed a few seconds to pull himself together.

He was getting better at it. And besides, he'd known this would be a tough day.

This was the first game since Mark's funeral.

The stands were filled with Ladder 177 guys and their families, all cheering for Mark's boys.

Lucas was helping out the new coach.

Some guys kept calling to Lucas from the stands.

Half the Jaguars had come, too. Lucas wasn't on the team anymore.

But he hadn't lost football. Or the guys.

He took a deep breath.

Yes, this would be a tough day — but a good one.

Dad had told Lucas it would get easier, as time passed.

He didn't mean *easy*. It meant that there would be minutes — like these — when he wasn't buried by sadness, when he wasn't stuck in the terror of that day in September. When he didn't think about the planes, or the thousands of people who'd died in the towers, or the faces of the men who'd planned the attacks.

The worst memories were from after he and Dad had escaped the dust, when they finally made it to the firehouse. Each hour had brought a new horror: the second tower collapsing, news that a plane had crashed into the Pentagon, outside Washington, D.C., and that another plane had been heading for the Capitol or the White House, but had crashed in Pennsylvania.

There was the moment when they found out about Mark.

Then Georgie.

Then Chief.

The other men had made it back, one by one. Covered in dust and ash. Some dripping with blood.

By that afternoon, there was only one man missing:

Uncle Benny.

The guys had seen him running into Tower 1, determined to get to the burning floors, to get as many people out as he could.

Lucas could see the doom in the eyes of the other men as they talked about Uncle Benny. But he'd sat on the floor of the firehouse, his eyes glued to the door.

Waiting.

Waiting.

Praying.

Dad had been right there with him.

That was one good thing that had come out of that day — Lucas and Dad.

They'd marched out of the dust holding hands and just kept on marching, together.

Last week Dad even brought the Seagrave model up from the basement.

The real rig was wrecked.

So Dad figured they should finish this one, and bring it to the firehouse. They worked on it some nights when neither of them could sleep. Sometimes Mom would sit with them. All they had to do now was paint it.

The score was tied in the fourth quarter. The other team called a time-out.

The kids all ran to the sidelines, surrounding their coach.

He stood there with his cane, his left arm in a sling, his shamrock tattoo peeping out from the top of the cast.

Uncle Benny.

"We have some champions here!" he boomed, turning to wink at Lucas.

Yes, Uncle Benny had made it out. He'd come down the stairs of the North Tower a minute before it collapsed, carrying a wounded man on his back. He got himself and the man under an engine truck and saved both of their lives.

He was in bad shape when he crawled out — shattered ankle, busted arm, collapsed lung. He was rushed to the hospital.

Word didn't reach the firehouse until early in the evening.

That is one memory that Lucas kept in his heart — the moment he heard that Uncle Benny was safe.

Lucas walked over as the kids ran back onto the field.

Uncle Benny had dropped his cane. So he leaned on Lucas as they stood and watched the kids play.

Their quarterback took the ball and then hurled it.

It was a terrible pass.

Impossible to catch.

But James took off after it.

The crowd stood and cheered.

Uncle Benny and Lucas laughed as they watched James go, go, go.

Mark's little boy ran with all of his might, his legs pumping, his arms reaching up, his face turned fearlessly toward the bright blue sky.

WHY I WROTE ABOUT SEPTEMBER 11

It was not part of my original plan to write about September 11, 2001, in the I Survived series. But over the past two years, I have received more than a thousand e-mails from kids asking me to write about this topic. At school visits, there are always kids who raise their hands and ask, "Will you be writing about 9/11?"

At first, my answer was always no. I was shocked that you would be so curious about that terrible day, which I had been trying to forget since it happened. I have friends who lost family members on 9/11 and others who narrowly escaped the towers before they collapsed. The memories of that day remain sharp and terrifying.

Though I work in New York City, in an office about a mile from the World Trade Center, I was not in New York City when the planes struck. I was *on* a plane above the Atlantic Ocean, heading back to New York from a family reunion and celebration in Europe. I had said good-bye to my husband in London; he was staying for a wedding of a business friend. I couldn't wait to see my kids and my parents, who would be waiting for me at a Little League game in our town, about thirty-five miles from New York City.

An hour and a half into the flight, I suddenly had the feeling that the plane was making a slow turn. Nobody else seemed to notice. I sat nervously, hoping I was imagining it. But then a stewardess made an announcement. "There has been a catastrophic event affecting all of North American airspace," she said. "We are returning to London. We will provide more information shortly."

Catastrophic event? The plane was silent as people tried to grasp what this could possibly mean. Earthquake? Bomb? One man actually thought a meteor could have hit somewhere in America. And then, moments later, the stewardess made another announcement.

"Ladies and gentlemen," she said. "I will now tell you what has occurred. . . ."

And for reasons I will never understand, she told our planeload of terrified people *exactly* what was happening: that planes had been hijacked by terrorists and flown into the World Trade Center and the Pentagon. There could be other planes involved, she said. The disaster was still unfolding.

An hour and a half later, we landed in London. Police escorted us into the chaotic airport. Somehow, I tracked down my husband. It wasn't until late that night that we were able to get a call through to our kids and my mom and dad. It was four days before flights started flying into the United States and we could get home.

What a sad and frightening time it was.

Thousands of firefighters and other rescue workers swarmed the sixteen-acre disaster zone, searching for survivors. The area, which became known as Ground Zero, was extremely dangerous. Underground fires smoldered, and the smoke was a toxic mix of melted plastic, steel, lead, and many poisonous chemicals. Few of the rescue workers had on proper protective clothing or masks.

And as it quickly became clear, there were not very many survivors to find. Only fourteen people were pulled out of the rubble alive, all within the first twenty-four hours of the collapse. About 50,000 people had been working in the buildings that day. Two thousand and sixteen died. Also among the dead: 343 firefighters and 60 police officers who were in or near the buildings when they collapsed.

In the months after the attacks, it was hard to imagine that life would ever go back to normal. It never will for many people, like my friend who lost her brother; like the hundreds of firefighters who have serious health problems caused by the toxic smoke and dust they breathed at Ground Zero; like the thousands who managed to escape that day, but who saw the horrors up close.

Today, while the horrors of that day still linger, the city itself is more vibrant than ever. People have done their best to move forward.

So why did I write this book?

Because after talking to many kids, teachers, and librarians, I began to understand why so many of you asked me to. September 11 shaped the world you were born into. It's only natural that you would be curious about it. I hope my story gives you a sense of that day — the fear and the courage, the sense of horror and shock.

I will admit that in my plans for this story, Uncle Benny did not survive the collapse of Tower 1. I even told my editor, Amanda, "Uncle Benny doesn't make it." She was sad to hear this, but we both agreed that this ending would be realistic. I had it in my mind that Uncle Benny had charged up the stairs of Tower 1, with fifty pounds of gear on his back, determined to get to the fire. Lucas waited for him to return to the firehouse, but he never did.

But as I wrote the last page of the last chapter of the book, with Lucas on the football field, suddenly there was Uncle Benny, standing with his crutches and his shamrock tattoo peeping out of his cast. I swear to you that he just *appeared*. I could picture him so clearly, still banged up, but his eyes sparkling, looking at me as if to say, "Come on, there was so much sadness that day. Could you please give Lucas's story a happy ending?"

And so I did.

Lauren Tarshis

TIME LINE FOR THE MORNING OF SEPTEMBER 11, 2001

8:46 A.M.: A commercial jet, American Airlines Flight 11, crashes into the North Tower (Tower 1) of the World Trade Center.

9:03 A.M.: Another jet, United Airlines Flight 175, crashes into the South Tower (Tower 2) of the World Trade Center.

9:37 A.M.: American Airlines Flight 77 crashes into the Pentagon, the headquarters of the United States military, in Arlington County, Virginia.

9:42 A.M.: United States airspace is shut down. No planes are allowed to take off and all aircraft in flight are ordered to land at the nearest airport.

9:59 A.M.: The South Tower of the World Trade Center begins to collapse. People from around

the country and the world watch
it on TV.

10:03 A.M.: A fourth and final jet,
United Airlines Flight 93, crashes
into a field in Shanksville,
Pennsylvania. It is later learned
that Flight 93 was intended for
either the United States Capitol
building or the White House in
Washington, D.C. Passengers on that
plane had learned of the crashes
at the World Trade Center and the
Pentagon. They stormed the cockpit
and tried to regain control of the
plane from the terrorists.

10:28 A.M.: The North Tower of the
World Trade Center collapses.

QUESTIONS AND ANSWERS ABOUT 9/11

Who committed the attacks?

The man mainly responsible for the attacks was named Osama bin Laden. He was the leader of a terrorist group called Al Qaeda. The group's headquarters was a rustic hideout in the country of Afghanistan. After a ten-year manhunt, bin Laden was discovered living in Pakistan, a country that borders Afghanistan. On May 2,

2011, Osama bin Laden was killed by SEAL Team 6, a special operations unit of the United States military.

How did the United States government react to the 9/11 attacks?

In the days after the attacks, President George W. Bush demanded that Afghanistan's government, run by a group called the Taliban, capture bin Laden and hand him over to the United States. The Taliban refused.

On October 7, 2001, the United States, joined by forces from other countries, declared war on Afghanistan. These forces toppled the Taliban government and captured or killed many members of Al Qaeda. Since 2001, more than 100,000 US soldiers have served in the Afghanistan War. As of 2012, there is a more democratic government leading Afghanistan, and our government is slowly withdrawing American troops.

What is at the World Trade Center now?

As of 2012, the World Trade Center was being completely rebuilt. Half of the land is covered by the National September 11 Memorial, which opened in September of 2011. It is a tribute to the nearly 3,000 people killed that day.

Where the Twin Towers once stood are now two enormous reflecting pools surrounded by two of the largest waterfalls in North America. The names of all of the victims are carved into bronze panels circling the Memorial pools. The pools arc surrounded by more than 400 oak trees, which will double in size in the next few years.

Underneath the memorial is the National 9/11 Memorial Museum, which is dedicated to exploring both the events of 9/11 and the lasting impact.

There will eventually be four buildings at the World Trade Center, including 1 World Trade Center, a 105-story-high skyscraper. When that building is complete, it will be the tallest building in the Western Hemisphere.

Do you have what it takes?

THE SINKING OF THE *TITANIC*, 1912

UNSINKABLE. UNTIL ONE NIGHT...

George Calder must be the luckiest kid alive. He and his little sister, Phoebe, are sailing with their aunt on the *Titanic*, the greatest ship ever built. George can't resist exploring every inch of the incredible boat, even if it keeps getting him into trouble.

Then the impossible happens — the *Titanic* hits an iceberg and water rushes in. George is stranded, alone and afraid, on the sinking ship. He's always gotten out of trouble before . . . but how can he survive this?

I SURVIVED

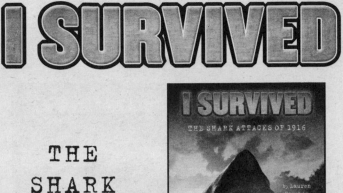

THE SHARK ATTACKS OF 1916

THERE'S SOMETHING IN THE WATER...

Chet Roscow is finally feeling at home in Elm Hills, New Jersey. He has a job with his uncle Jerry at the local diner, three great friends, and the perfect summer-time destination: cool, refreshing Matawan Creek.

But Chet's summer is interrupted by shocking news. A great white shark has been attacking swimmers along the Jersey shore, not far from Elm Hills. Everyone in town is talking about it. So when Chet sees something in the creek, he's sure it's his imagination . . . until he comes face-to-face with a bloodthirsty shark!

I SURVIVED

HURRICANE KATRINA, 2005

HIS WHOLE WORLD IS UNDERWATER...

Barry's family tries to evacuate before Hurricane Katrina hits their home in the Lower Ninth Ward of New Orleans. But when Barry's little sister gets terribly sick, they're forced to stay home and wait out the storm.

At first, Katrina doesn't seem to be as severe a storm as forecasters predicted. But overnight the levees break, and Barry's world is literally torn apart. He's swept away by the floodwaters, away from his family. Can he survive the storm of the century — alone?

I SURVIVED

THE BOMBING OF PEARL HARBOR, 1941

A DAY NO ONE WILL EVER FORGET...

Ever since Danny's mom moved him to Hawaii, away from the dangerous streets of New York City, Danny has been planning to go back. He's not afraid of the crime or the dark alleys. And he's not afraid to stow away on the next ship out of Pearl Harbor.

But that morning, the skies fill with fighter planes. Bombs pound the harbor. Bullets rain down on the beaches. Danny is shocked — and, for the first time, he is truly afraid. He's a tough city kid. But can Danny survive the day that will live in infamy?

I SURVIVED

THE SAN FRANCISCO EARTHQUAKE, 1906

A CITY ON THE RISE — SUDDENLY FALLS...

Leo loves being a newsboy in San Francisco — he needs the money but the job also gives him the freedom to explore the amazing, hilly city as it changes and grows with the new century. Horse-drawn carriages share the streets with shiny automobiles, businesses and families move in every day from everywhere, and anything seems possible.

But early one spring morning, everything changes. Leo's world is shaken — literally — and he finds himself stranded in the middle of San Francisco as it crumbles and burns to the ground. Can Leo survive this devastating disaster?